127737

Puffin Books, Penguin Books Ltd, Harmondsworth, Middlesex, England
Viking Penguin Inc., 40 West 23rd Street, New York, New York 10010, U.S.A.
Penguin Books Australia Ltd, Ringwood, Victoria, Australia
Penguin Books Canada Ltd, 2801 John Street, Markham, Ontario, Canada L3R 1B4
Penguin Books (N.Z.) Ltd, 182-190 Wairau Road, Auckland 10, New Zealand

First published by Ernest Benn Limited 1981
First published 1987 in Pocket Puffins
by Puffin Books in association with Moonlight Publishing Ltd
Copyright © Helen Oxenbury, 1981

Made and printed in Italy by Editoriale Libraria

BILL
AND STANLEY

by Helen Oxenbury

Bill ate up all his cabbage
to please his mum.
"Now she will *have*
to play with me,"
he thought.

"I'm much too busy,"
said Bill's mum.
"Go in the garden
and play on your own for a bit."

"She's always busy,"
thought Bill.
"No-one ever plays with me."—
but he was wrong.

Stanley did.

They rolled in the long grass, until Stanley found a ball.

"Throw it," said Bill; but Stanley wouldn't.

Bill wanted to hide
chocolate drops
for Stanley to find;
Stanley couldn't wait.

So they balanced
on top of a wall.

They made tea.
"What do you fancy Stanley?
Currant cake?"

Then they played army games...

…then pirates,
until they were tired out

So they had a little rest
but soon
it was time for supper.

"There.
You *can* play on your own,"
said his mother.